JESUS *of* NAZARETH

A LIFE OF CHRIST THROUGH PICTURES

ILLUSTRATED WITH PAINTINGS FROM
THE NATIONAL GALLERY OF ART, WASHINGTON, D.C.

SIMON & SCHUSTER BOOKS FOR YOUNG READERS
Published by Simon & Schuster
New York London Toronto Sydney Tokyo Singapore
in association with the National Gallery of Art, Washington, D.C.

INTRODUCTION

The following pages depict the life of Jesus in both words and pictures. The text consists of excerpts from the King James Version of the Bible, and the illustrations of paintings by European artists who lived between the fourteenth and seventeenth centuries.

Because Jesus' physical appearance is not described in the New Testament gospels, artists have had to rely on their own imagination and pictorial traditions when depicting scenes from his life. Since relatively few people could read during this period, pictures often served as teaching tools. In order to make Jesus' life more accessible, artists often included details that would have been easily recognizable from everyday life. In turn, today, the clothes, buildings, and backgrounds in these paintings often give us clues as to the appearance of the artists' own world.

Typically, rich patrons would pay an artist to paint a particular scene from Christ's life and then hang the artwork in a favorite church. People considered these paintings as both a gift to God and as an aid to prayer for those who came to worship.

The words come from the King James Version of the Bible, a seventeeth-century translation of the scriptures from Latin into English. People have used this version since the time of Shakespeare and the Pilgrim Fathers, and the language in which the story is told has helped to shape the way we think of Jesus.

As you turn the pages of this book, words and paintings will take you from the annunciation of Jesus' birth, through his boyhood, the events of his ministry, his crucifixion, and ascension into heaven. Each painting is a triumph of skill and imagination.

JOY RICHARDSON

The NATIVITY

Jesus is born in Bethlehem where Joseph and Mary have gone to pay their taxes.

And it came to pass in those days, that there went out a decree from Caesar Augustus that all the world should be taxed. And all went to be taxed, every one into his own city. And Joseph also went up from Galilee, out of the city of Nazareth, into Judea, unto the city of David, which is called Bethlehem, to be taxed with Mary his espoused wife, being great with child.

And so it was that, while they were there, the days were accomplished that she should be delivered. And she brought forth her firstborn son, and wrapped him in swaddling clothes and laid him in a manger, because there was no room for them in the inn.

LUKE 2

The FLIGHT *into* EGYPT

After three wise men tell King Herod that Jesus is the King of the Jews, Herod orders his soldiers to find and kill the newborn baby.

And behold, the angel of the Lord appeareth to Joseph in a dream, saying, "Arise, and take the young child and his mother, and flee into Egypt, and be thou there until I bring thee word: for Herod will seek the young child to destroy him."

When he arose, he took the young child and his mother by night, and departed into Egypt, and was there until the death of Herod.

But when Herod was dead, behold, an angel of the Lord appeareth in a dream to Joseph in Egypt, saying, "Arise, and take the young child and his mother, and go into the land of Israel, for they are dead which sought the young child's life."

And he came and dwelt in a city called Nazareth.

MATTHEW 2

The FINDING *in the* TEMPLE

When Jesus is twelve, he travels with his parents to Jerusalem for the feast of the passover.

And when they fulfilled the days, as they returned, the child Jesus tarried behind in Jerusalem; and Joseph and his mother knew not of it. But they, supposing him to have been in the company, went a day's journey; and they sought him among their kinsfolk and acquaintance. And when they found him not, they turned back again to Jerusalem, seeking him.

And it came to pass that after three days they found him in the temple, sitting in the midst of the doctors, both hearing them and asking them questions. And all that heard him were astonished at his understanding and answers.

And Jesus increased in wisdom and stature, and in favor with God and man.

LUKE 2

The BAPTISM *of* JESUS

After Jesus becomes an adult, he is baptized by his cousin, John the Baptist.

In those days came John the Baptist, preaching in the wilderness of Judea, and saying, "Repent ye, for the kingdom of heaven is at hand."

Then went out to him Jerusalem and all Judea and all the region round about Jordan, and were baptized of him in Jordan, confessing their sins.

Then cometh Jesus from Galilee to Jordan unto John, to be baptized of him. But John forbade him, saying, "I have need to be baptized of thee, and comest thou to me?" And Jesus, answering, said unto him, "Suffer it to be so now."

And Jesus, when he was baptized, went up straightway out of the water, and lo, the heavens were opened unto him and he saw the Spirit of God descending like a dove, and lighting upon him; and lo, a voice from heaven, saying, "This is my beloved Son, in whom I am well pleased."

MATTHEW 3

The TEMPTATION *in the* WILDERNESS

Jesus spends forty days in the wilderness where he is tested by the devil.

And Jesus being full of the Holy Ghost returned from Jordan and was led by the Spirit into the wilderness. And the devil said unto him, "If thou be the Son of God, command this stone that it be made bread."

And Jesus answered him, saying, "It is written that man shall not live by bread alone, but by every word from God."

And when the devil had ended all the temptation, he departed from him for a season. And Jesus returned in the power of the Spirit into Galilee: and there went out a fame of him through all the region round about.

LUKE 4

The CALLING *of* PETER *and* ANDREW

When Herod hears that John is baptizing people, he throws him into prison.

Peter and Andrew become Jesus' disciples.

Now when Jesus had heard that John was cast into prison, he departed into Galilee. From that time Jesus began to preach, and to say, "Repent, for the kingdom of heaven is at hand."

And Jesus, walking by the sea of Galilee, saw two brethren, Simon called Peter and Andrew his brother, casting a net into the sea: for they were fishers.

And he saith unto them, "Follow me, and I will make you fishers of men."

And they straightway left their nets and followed him.

MATTHEW 4

PLENA DOMINVS TECV
ET DENEDICTVS

The MARRIAGE *at* CANA

Jesus performs his first miracle.

And the third day there was a marriage in Cana of Galilee; and the mother of Jesus was there. And when they wanted wine, the mother of Jesus saith unto him, "They have no wine." Jesus saith unto her, "Woman, what have I to do with thee? Mine hour is not yet come." His mother saith unto the servants, "Whatsoever he saith unto you, do it."

And there were set there six waterpots of stone, containing two or three firkins apiece. Jesus saith unto them, "Fill the waterpots with water." And they filled them up to the brim.

When the ruler of the feast had tasted the water that was made wine, and knew not whence it was (but the servants which drew the water knew), the governor of the feast called the bridegroom and saith unto him, "Every man at the beginning doth set forth good wine; and when men have well drunk, then that which is worse; but thou hast kept the good wine until now."

This beginning of miracles did Jesus in Cana of Galilee, and manifested forth his glory; and his disciples believed on him.

JOHN 2

And Jesus going up to Jerusalem took the twelve disciples apart in the way, and said unto them, "Behold, we go up to Jerusalem; and the Son of man shall be betrayed unto the chief priests and unto the scribes, and they shall condemn him to death."

And Jesus went into the temple of God and cast out all them that sold and bought in the temple, and overthrew the tables of the moneychangers and the seats of them that sold doves, and said unto them, "It is written, 'My house shall be called the house of prayer'; but ye have made it a den of thieves."

And the blind and the lame came to him in the temple, and he healed them.

MATTHEW 20, 21

The CLEANSING *of the* TEMPLE

Jesus drives the money changers and merchants from the temple in Jerusalem.

The LAST SUPPER

Jesus has his last meal with his disciples before his arrest.
It was at this meal that he instituted the celebration of the Eucharist.

Now the first day of the feast of unleavened bread the disciples came to Jesus, saying unto him, "Where wilt thou that we prepare for thee to eat the passover?" And he said, "Go into the city to such a man and say unto him, 'The master saith, My time is at hand; I will keep the passover at thy house with my disciples.' " And the disciples did as Jesus had appointed them; and they made ready the passover.

Now when the even was come, he sat down with the twelve. And as they did eat, he said, "Verily I say unto you, that one of you shall betray me."

And they were exceedingly sorrowful, and began every one of them to say unto him, "Lord, is it I?" And he answered, "He that dippeth his hand with me in the dish, the same shall betray me."

Then Judas, which betrayed him, answered, "Master, is it I?" He said unto him, "Thou hast said."

And when they had sung a hymn, they went out into the mount of Olives.

MATTHEW 26

The AGONY *in the* GARDEN

Jesus prays that he might be spared imminent suffering and death.

And they came to a place which was named Gethsemane; and he saith to his disciples, "Sit ye here, while I shall pray." And he taketh with him Peter and James and John, and began to be sore amazed and to be very heavy; and saith unto them, "My soul is exceeding sorrowful unto death; tarry ye here, and watch."

And he went forward a little, and fell on the ground and prayed that, if it were possible, the hour might pass from him. And he said, "Abba, Father, all things are possible unto thee; take away this cup from me; nevertheless not what I will, but what thou wilt."

And he cometh, and findeth them sleeping, and saith unto Peter, "Simon, sleepest thou? Couldest not thou watch one hour?" And again he went away and prayed, and spake the same words. And when he returned, he found them asleep again (for their eyes were heavy). And he cometh the third time, and saith unto them, "Sleep on now, and take your rest; it is enough, the hour is come. Rise up, and let us go; lo, he that betrayeth me is at hand."

MARK 14

·I·N·R·I·

The CRUCIFIXION

Jesus is arrested and brought before Pontius Pilate, the governor of Judea, who delivers him to be crucified.

And they bring him unto the place Golgotha, which is, being interpreted, The place of a skull. And it was the third hour, and they crucified him. And the superscription of his accusation was written over, THE KING OF THE JEWS. And with him they crucify two thieves; the one on his right hand, and the other on his left.

And when the sixth hour was come, there was darkness over the whole land until the ninth hour. And at the ninth hour Jesus cried with a loud voice, saying, "Eloi, Eloi, lama sabachthani?" which is, being interpreted, "My God, my God, why hast thou forsaken me?"

And Jesus cried with a loud voice, and gave up the ghost.

And when the centurion, which stood over against him, saw that he so cried out and gave up the ghost, he said, "Truly this man was the Son of God."

MARK 15

The BURIAL *and* RESURRECTION

Jesus rises from the dead on the third day after his crucifixion.

When the even was come, there came a rich man of Arimathea, named Joseph, who also himself was Jesus' disciple; he went to Pilate and begged the body of Jesus. Then Pilate commanded the body to be delivered.

And when Joseph had taken the body, he wrapped it in a clean linen cloth, and laid it in his own new tomb, which he had hewn out in the rock.

In the end of the sabbath, as it began to dawn toward the first day of the week, came Mary Magdalene and the other Mary to see the sepulchre.

And behold, there was a great earthquake; for the angel of the Lord descended from heaven and came and rolled back the stone from the door, and sat upon it. And the angel said unto the women, "Fear not ye; for I know that ye seek Jesus, which was crucified. He is not here; for he has risen, as he said."

MATTHEW 27, 28

The ASCENSION *into* HEAVEN

Forty days later, Jesus appears before his disciples and Mary, his mother.

And being assembled together with them, [he] commanded them that they should not depart from Jerusalem, but wait for the promise of the Father, "which," saith he, "ye have heard of me."

And when he had spoken these things, while they beheld, he was taken up; and a cloud received him out of their sight.

ACTS 1

INDEX *to* PAINTINGS

The illustrations are details of the following paintings.

(ABOVE) *Front cover and page 19*
The Calling of the Apostles Peter and Andrew
DUCCIO DI BUONINSEGNA
(Sienese, about 1255–1318)
Swimming in the Sea of Galilee are an octopus, lobster, eel, ray and many kinds of fish. As fishermen, the brothers catch all kinds of creatures. Symbolically, as apostles they convert all kinds of humans.

(ABOVE) *Page 5 (title page)*
The Annunciation
FILIPPO LIPPI
(Florentine, about 1406–1469)
This panel's unusual shape suggests that it was meant to be installed above a doorway in a Gothic building with steep arches. The room is filled with bright sunshine—or perhaps with heavenly light, accompanying the appearance of the angel.

(ABOVE) *Page 8*
The Adoration of the Shepherds
ADRIAEN ISENBRANT
(Bruges, active 1510–1551)
By positioning Jesus above the crib—instead of in it—the artist gives the crib the appearance of an altar. One peasant plays a bladder pipe to amuse the baby. On a far-off hill, peasants dance around a bonfire, recalling the wintry Christmas season.

(ABOVE) *Page 4 (opposite title page)*
Madonna and Child with Saints in the Enclosed Garden
FOLLOWER OF ROBERT CAMPIN
(Netherlandish, 15th century)
A garden wall shelters the holy people from the outside world. Symbols from their legends identify the saints: Catherine, a wheel and a sword; John the Baptist, a lamb; Barbara, a tower; and Anthony Abbot, a pig.

(LEFT) *Back cover and page 7 (introduction)*
The Annunciation
MASTER OF THE BARBERINI PANELS
(Umbrian-Florentine, active 3rd quarter 15th century)
The dove of the Holy Ghost flies down from heaven. The vase of roses refers to Mary's purity. The artist gives the scene a sense of depth by using "linear perspective." This effect is achieved through the converging lines of the floor and buildings.

(BELOW) *Page 9*
The Adoration of the Magi
BOTTICELLI
(Florentine, 1444 or 1445–1510)
Following tradition, the three Wise Men are composed of a young man, a mature man, and an old man, indicating that men of all ages worshiped Jesus. The ruins of an ancient temple, now used as a stable, suggest the victorious overthrow of pagan beliefs by Christianity.

(ABOVE) *Page 10*
Madonna and Child and the Infant Saint John in a Landscape
POLIDORO LANZANI
(Venetian, 1515–1565)
Although the Bible does not mention that Jesus and his cousin John the Baptist met before the two were adults, artists have repeatedly chosen to celebrate Jesus' humanity by depicting them together as children.

(BELOW) *Page 11*
The Rest on the Flight into Egypt
GERARD DAVID
(Netherlandish, about 1460–1523)
Mary holds grapes for Jesus to eat while, in the background, Joseph beats chestnuts from a tree. The cool blue and green landscape creates a quiet mood, reassuring the viewer that the Holy Family is now safe.

(ABOVE) *Page 12*
Christ among the Doctors
BERNHARD VAN ORLEY
(Netherlandish, about 1488–1541)
Behind the sitting figure of Jesus are Joseph and Mary, who stand in a street with brick houses typical of northern Europe. Artists sometimes placed religious events in familiar settings to give the stories a more immediate impact.

(ABOVE) *Page 13*
Christ among the Doctors
MASTER OF THE CATHOLIC KINGS
(Hispano-Flemish, active late 15th century)
Jesus' gesture suggests he's making a point during debate. The panel comes from an altarpiece painted for Spain's monarchs Ferdinand and Isabella. The unknown artist is named after this work.

(RIGHT) *Page 14*
The Baptism of Christ
JUAN DE FLANDES
(Hispano-Flemish, active 1496–1519)
God the Father, wearing the triple crown of a pope, appears in the sky with the sun and crescent moon. This large altarpiece panel is by the same painter as the tiny ***Temptation*** on page 16.

(ABOVE) *Page 15*
The Baptism of Christ
MASTER OF THE LIFE OF SAINT JOHN THE BAPTIST
(Rimini, active 2nd quarter 14th century)
The gold-leaf background symbolizes divine light. God appears in the sky, while two angels hold Jesus' robes. John the Baptist wears camel skins, reminding us that he lived his life as a hermit in the desert.

(ABOVE) *Page 16*
The Temptation of Christ
Juan de Flandes
(Hispano-Flemish, active 1496-1519)
The devil, although dressed as a monk, has horns and lizard feet. Only eight inches high, this picture was one of forty-seven tiny scenes painted for Spain's Queen Isabella depicting the lives of Jesus and Mary.

(BELOW) *Pages 18 and 29*
The Crucifixion with Saint Jerome and Saint Francis
Pesellino
(Florentine, 1422-1457)
Jerome is depicted with a stone in his hand because as an act of penance he repeatedly beat his chest. Golden rays mark the Christlike wounds on Francis's hands and feet. The flaming sun and black moon recall the terrifying events that, according to the Bible, took place when Jesus died.

(ABOVE) *Pages 20 and 21*
The Marriage at Cana
Master of the Catholic Kings
(Hispano-Flemish, active late 15th century)
This painting, and the one shown on page 13, formed parts of an altarpiece that was probably painted in commemoration of a royal wedding in 1497. Shields hanging from the rafters bear coats of arms of Spain and the Holy Roman Empire.

(ABOVE) *page 22*
Christ Cleansing the Temple
El Greco
(Spanish, 1541-1615)
On the floor of the Temple in Jerusalem, a child is playing with coins rather than praying. Among the animals and birds being sold are a lamb, symbolic of Jesus, and white doves, referring to the Holy Ghost.

(ABOVE) *Page 25*
The Last Supper
William Blake
(British, 1757-1827)
Jesus, his disciples, and Mary Magdalene celebrate the Last Supper. In the lower right corner, Judas counts his silver even though the Bible implies he was not paid until after the betrayal.

(LEFT) *Pages 17 and 23*
The Baptism of Christ
Master of Saint Bartholomew Altar
(German, active about 1475-1510)
Jesus, his cousin John, and attendant angels gather by the River Jordan. The baptism takes place in a landscape setting with blue sky, while from a golden heaven God the Father and fourteen saints witness the event.

(RIGHT) *Page 28*
The Crucifixion
Paolo Veneziano
(Venetian, documented 1333-1358/1362)
Mary faints into the arms of holy women as a Roman soldier raises his hand, saluting Jesus as the Son of God. Mary Magdalene kneels beside a bloody skull, while angels collect Christ's blood in golden goblets.

(ABOVE) *Page 27*
The Agony in the Garden
BENVENUTO DI GIOVANNI
(Sienese, 1436-about 1518)
Holding a sacred chalice, a glowing angel appears to Jesus as he prays, but the apostles have fallen asleep instead of praying with him.

(LEFT) *Page 30*
The Crucifixion
SANO DI PIETRO
(Sienese, 1406-1481)
With stark simplicity, a single holy figure is placed on either side of Jesus' cross. His mother sits with her hands clasped in prayer, while his friend John the Evangelist grieves.

(RIGHT) *Page 31*
The Lamentation
ANDREA SOLARIO
(Milanese, active 1495-1524)
As Mary holds her son's body on her lap, John the Evangelist looks out at viewers, asking us to share their grief. On the distant hilltop, Christ's cross stands empty between those of the two thieves.

(RIGHT) *Pages 32 and 33*
The Ascension
JOHANN KOERBECKE
(German, about 1420-1491)
As Jesus rises into a golden heaven, he is greeted by eight Old Testament figures. Some of the apostles stare in amazement at Christ's footprints in the rock, while John the Evangelist comforts Mary.

SIMON & SCHUSTER
BOOKS FOR YOUNG READERS
1230 Avenue of the Americas, New York, New York 10020. First Published in Great Britain in 1994 by Frances Lincoln Limited, 4 Torriano Mews, Torriano Avenue, London NW5 2RZ. Designed by David Fordham. The text of this book is set in Berkeley Book. Manufactured in Italy.

10 9 8 7 6 5 4 3 2 1

Library of Congress Cataloging-in-Publication Data
Jesus of Nazareth : illustrated with paintings from the National Gallery in Washington.
p. cm. Includes index. 1. Jesus Christ—Biography—Juvenile literature. [1. Jesus Christ—Biography. 2. Jesus Christ—Art.] I. National Gallery of Art (U.S.) BT302.J574 1994 232.9'01—dc20 [B] 93-35867 CIP AC
ISBN: 0-671-88651-7